D0553787

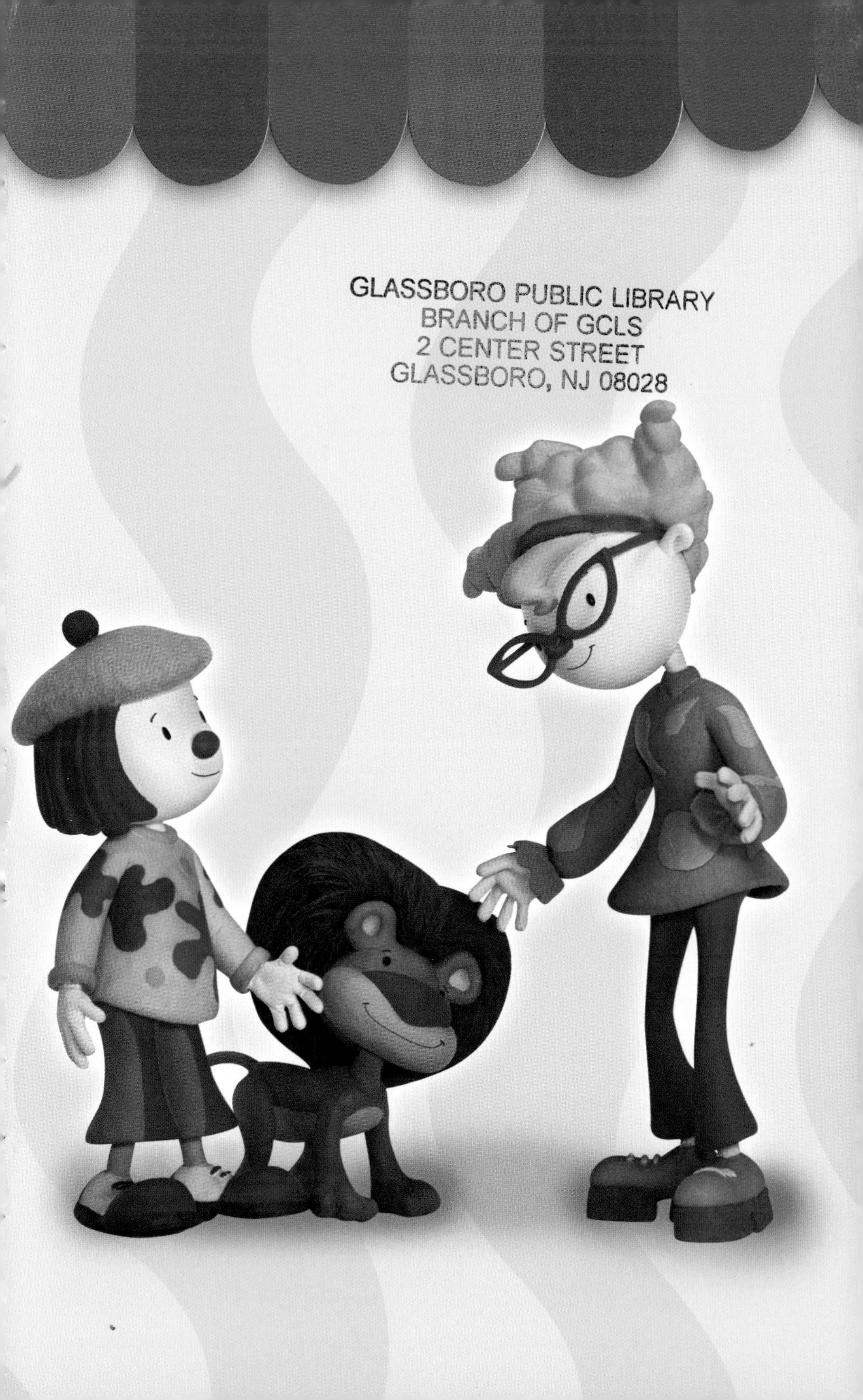

Printed in the United States of America

First Edition
1 3 5 7 9 10 8 6 4 2

Library of Congress Catalog Card Number on file

ISBN 0-7868-4680-1

For more Disney Press fun, visit www.disneybooks.com

Clown School

By Tennant Redbank

Disney PRESS

New York

Hi!
I am JoJo.

I am going to school.
Do you want to come?
Clown school is cool!

It is time to go!
We cannot be late.
This is my class.
It is so great!

Our teacher tells us
what we need to know.
Like how to be silly
when we put on a show.

We do tricks
all morning long.

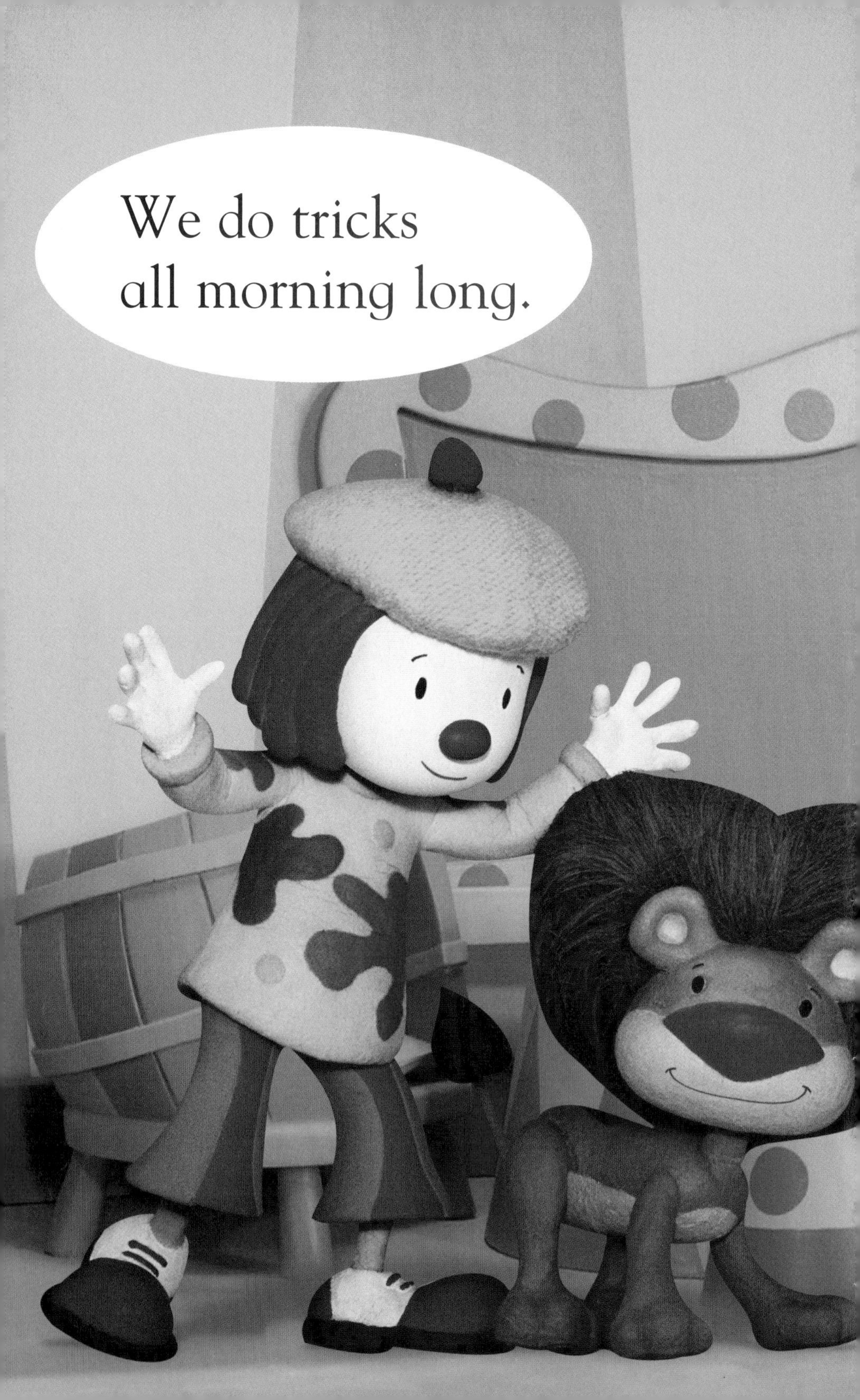

Then we learn jokes
or sing a song.

Skeebo makes a face.

Trina walks a wire.

Tater falls asleep.

Croaky swings up higher.

Then we juggle.
It is really fun!
I am pretty good,
except when I drop one.

Making people laugh
is the best part.
It is why I am a clown.

And I try
with all my heart.